THE LAZIES

THE LAZIES

Tales of the
Peoples of Russia

Translated and Edited by
MIRRA GINSBURG

Illustrated by Marian Parry

Macmillan Publishing Co., Inc.
New York

10   9   8   7   6   5   4   3   2   1

Library of Congress Cataloging in Publication Data

Ginsburg, Mirra, comp.
      The lazies.

          CONTENTS: Sheidulla.—Who will wash the pot?—Easy
bread. [etc.]
          1. Tales, Russian. [1. Folklore—Russia]
I. Parry, Marian, illus. II. Title.
PZ8.1.G455 Laz   398.2'0947   72-92437 ISBN 0-02-735840-2

Three oranges fell from the sky—
one for the teller of these tales,
another for the listener,
and the third for everybody else.

Contents

THE LAZIES

Sheidulla

AN AZERBAIDZHAN TALE

Sheidulla was the laziest man in his village. His wife and children were always hungry and were dressed in rags. His roof leaked, his fence was broken. But he would do nothing all day long except lie under a tree and sleep. His wife cried and scolded, and begged him to go to work, but Sheidulla had one answer:

"Don't worry, wife. We are poor today, but one day we'll be rich and happy."

"How can we get rich if you don't work?" his wife would ask. "You lie around all day and will not lift a finger."

But Sheidulla kept repeating:

"Wait, we'll be rich, the time will come."

His wife waited, his children waited, but the time never came.

"We have waited enough," said his wife. "If you don't do something, we shall die of hunger."

So Sheidulla decided to pay a visit to the wise man and ask him how to rid himself of poverty.

He bade his wife and children good-by, and set off on the journey. He walked a day, two days, three days. And then he met a lean, starved wolf.

"Where are you going, good man?" asked the wolf.

"I am going to the wise man. Perhaps he will tell me how to get rich."

When he heard this, the wolf said to Sheidulla:

"Do me a favor, find out from the wise man what I can do. For three years now I've had a terrible stomach ache, and I can't get rid of it. Perhaps he will tell you of a cure for my pain."

"Very well," said Sheidulla. "I'll ask him."

And he went on. Again he walked three days and three

nights, until he came to an apple tree by the roadside.

"Where are you going, good man?" asked the apple tree.

"I am going to the wise man to find out how to get rich without working."

"Do me a favor," begged the apple tree. "Every spring I am covered with blossoms, but as soon as they open, they drop, and I never bear a single apple. Ask the wise man what can be done about it."

"Very well," said Sheidulla. "I'll ask him."

And he went on. Again he walked three days and three nights, until he came to a deep lake. An enormous fish raised its head above the water and asked:

"Where are you going, good man?"

"I am going to the wise man for advice on how to get rich."

"Do me a favor, ask him something for me too. For seven years now I've had a sore throat, as though something were stuck there. Perhaps he will tell you what to do for it."

"Very well," said Sheidulla. "I'll ask him."

And he went on. Again he walked three days and three nights, until he came to a beautiful rose garden. Under one of the rose bushes sat an old, old man with a long white beard. The old man looked up at Sheidulla and asked:

"What brings you here, Sheidulla?"

"How did you know my name?" Sheidulla cried out in amazement. "Are you the wise man I am looking for?"

"I am," the old man said. "What do you want of me?"

And so Sheidulla told him about his troubles and asked for his advice.

The wise man listened patiently, then he said:

"Is there anything else you wish to ask me?"

"There is," said Sheidulla. And he told him about the requests of the lean wolf, the apple tree, and the huge fish.

"That fish," said the wise man, "has a large, precious diamond stuck in its throat. When the diamond is removed, the fish will recover. Under the apple tree lies buried a pot of gold. When the pot is dug out, the blossoms will no longer

4

drop and the tree will bear fruit. And the wolf will be cured of his pain when he swallows the first lazy man he meets."

"And what about my request?" asked Sheidulla.

"Your request is already fulfilled. You may go."

Sheidulla rejoiced and turned homeward. He walked and walked until he reached the lake. The fish was waiting for him anxiously.

"What did the wise man say?" it cried.

"There is a precious diamond stuck in your throat. As soon as it's removed, your pain will disappear," Sheidulla answered and turned to go on.

"Kind man, take pity on me," the fish began to plead. "Take out the diamond. You'll free me of the pain, and will get rich yourself."

"Oh, no! Why should I bother? The wise man said that my request has been granted. Wealth will come to me of itself," said Sheidulla, and went on until he came to the apple tree.

When the apple tree saw him, all its branches, all its leaves began to quiver.

"Well, well," it cried. "Did the wise man tell you how to end my affliction?"

"He did," said Sheidulla. "There is a large pot of gold

5

buried under your roots. When the gold is removed, you'll bear the tastiest apples in the world."

And he turned to go on.

But the apple tree begged him:

"Dig out the pot of gold from under my roots. I will be happy, and you will be rewarded too. You'll get rich all at once."

"Oh, no! Why should I bother? I will have everything without your gold," said Sheidulla, and went on.

He walked and he walked until he met the lean wolf. When the wolf saw him, he shook with impatience.

"Well, well," he cried. "What did the wise man say? But hurry, don't make me wait!"

"If you will swallow the first lazy man you meet, you will get well at once," said Sheidulla.

The wolf thanked him kindly, and began to ask about his journey, about everything he had seen and heard on the way. Sheidulla told him about his meeting with the fish and with the apple tree, and what they had asked him. The wolf listened carefully and said:

"And did you get the precious stone and the pot of gold?"

"Ha!" cried Sheidulla. "Why should I have bothered? I'll be rich without them."

"Well, now," the wolf said with a laugh. "There is no need

for me to search for a lazy man—he has come to me himself. There's no one in the world who is lazier and more stupid than Sheidulla."

And with these words the wolf leaped upon him, and in one gulp he swallowed him, shoes and all. And that was the end of the lazy Sheidulla.

Who Will Wash the Pot?

A RUSSIAN TALE

Not so long ago there lived an old man and his wife. Both were very lazy. One day the old man said:

"Cook us some cereal, old woman."

She moaned, and she groaned, and then she said:

"All right, old man, I will."

She cooked the cereal. It was good, and they ate it all up. But neither wanted to wash the pot. The old man said to the old woman:

"You wash it!"

And the old woman said:

"You wash it!"

They argued all day, and the pot was still dirty. Then they went to sleep, and the pot was still dirty. The old man said:

"Whoever speaks first in the morning, that one will wash the pot."

In the morning they woke up, and the pot was still dirty.

And they both stayed in bed, and he did not speak and she did not speak.

The day passed, and evening came. They did not get up, they did not fire the stove, they did not cook, they did not eat, and they did not speak.

The neighbors saw no smoke coming up from their chimney and came in to see what was wrong. They asked:

"Are you sick?"

But neither one answered.

They asked:

"What happened?"

But neither one answered.

Then the neighbors called the mayor of the village. He spoke to the old man, he spoke to the old woman.

Neither one answered.

"Something is wrong," said the mayor. "One of you must stay here and look after them."

"I will," said a woman. "But who will pay me?"

"There's a new coat hanging on the nail," said the mayor. "Take that as payment for your work."

"What?" screamed the old woman, and jumped out of bed. "Nobody's going to take away my coat!"

And the old man turned around and said:

"You wash the pot."

Easy Bread

A BYELORUSSIAN TALE

A peasant was working in the field. He worked till he got tired. Then he sat down under a bush, untied his sack, took out a piece of bread, and began to eat.

At that moment a hungry wolf came out of the woods.

"What are you eating, man?" he asked.

"Bread," the peasant answered.

"How does it taste?"

"Delicious."

"Let me try a piece."

The peasant broke off a piece and gave it to the wolf.

"It's good," said the wolf. "I wish I had some every day. But how can I get it? Won't you tell me, man?"

"Why not?" said the peasant. "I'll teach you how to get it."

And he began:

"First you plow the land. . . ."

"And then I'll have bread?"

"Wait a while. Next you must sow the rye. . . ."

"And then I'll have bread?"

"Not so quick. Now you must wait until it grows, and blossoms, and forms ears, and ripens. . . ."

"Such a long wait," said the wolf with a sigh. "But after that I'll eat my fill?"

"Not yet," the peasant said. "It's still too soon. When it ripens, the rye must be harvested, tied up in sheaves, and stacked. The wind will winnow it, the sun will dry it. . . ."

"And then I'll have my bread?"

"Not so fast, friend! The sheaves have to be threshed, the grain poured into sacks and taken to the mill, to be ground into flour. . . ."

"And then it's ready?"

"Not just yet. You'll have to mix the flour into dough and wait until it rises. And when it's risen, you shape it into loaves and put them into the oven."

"And the bread will be baked?"

"Yes, then it will be baked, and you can have your fill of it."

The wolf thought awhile, scratched his head, and said:

"No, come to think of it, that's too much trouble. You'd better tell me how to get easier bread."

"Well," said the peasant. "If you won't work for your food,

go out into the meadow. A horse is grazing there, he may be easier to get."

The wolf went to the meadow and saw the horse.

"Horse, horse, I'm going to eat you."

"You're welcome," said the horse. "But first take the shoes off my hooves. They're made of iron, and you may break your teeth on them."

The wolf bent down to remove the shoes, and the horse gave him such a kick that he turned a somersault and ran off whimpering to look for easier food.

He came to a riverbank and saw a flock of geese in the grass:

"Geese, geese," he said. "I'm going to eat you."

"You're welcome," said the geese. "But do us one last favor."

"And what is that?"

"We've heard so much about your voice. Sing us a song before we die."

The wolf sat down on his haunches, raised his head, and let out a long, long howl. Meantime, the geese went flap, flap with their wings, rose up into the air, and off they flew.

The wolf looked after them, shook his head, and then went on, scolding himself.

"I won't be fooled again," he said. "I will eat the next creature I meet."

Just as he said it, he saw an old man coming down the road. The wolf ran up to him:

"Grandpa, grandpa, I'm going to eat you!"

"You're welcome," said the old man. "But what's the hurry? Let's have a smoke before your meal."

"Is it pleasant?"

"Try it, you'll see."

The old man took out his tobacco pouch, rolled a cigarette, lit it, and took a puff. Then he gave it to the wolf. The

wolf got his lungs full of smoke and started choking and coughing, tears running from his eyes until he couldn't see a thing. And by the time he had finished coughing, the old man was safely back in his village.

"I don't seem to be doing so well," the wolf said to himself. Then he went on until he met a kid.

"Kid, kid, I'm going to eat you!"

But the kid said:

"Why, you are welcome. But before you eat me, let me say good-by to my poor mother. She's just over that hill."

And when the wolf came near the mother goat, she leaped and tore into his side with her sharp horns. He flew over the hilltop and went rolling down, over and over, until the whole world turned before his eyes. And when he finally reached the bottom, he shook his head and said:

"Now, did I eat the kid or didn't I?"

Just then the peasant, who had finished his day's work, was passing by. He heard the wolf and laughed.

"Well, that you didn't. But you surely had your fill of easy bread."

Who Will Row Next?

AN EVENK TALE

Three village women decided to go fishing in the river with a net. They went to the old man who lived next door and said:

"We have a net, you have boat. Let's go fishing together."

"I'd like to eat some fresh fish," said the old man. "But I've grown old and weak, I have no strength to row any more."

"You will not need to row," said the women. "We'll take turns. You won't have to do anything but steer."

"In that case I will come," the old man agreed.

They got into the boat and rowed upstream. The youngest woman was the first to row.

When they came to the first brook flowing into the river, the middle woman took the oars. They went on and on until they came to the second brook. Now it was the eldest woman's turn to row.

They went on and on until they came to the third brook. The eldest woman put down the oars, and no one picked them up. The boat stopped, rocking on the waves.

18

"Well?" asked the old man. "The fishing place is after the fourth brook. Why don't you row? Whose turn is it?"

"I don't know whose turn it is," said the eldest woman. "But mine is finished."

"So is mine," said the middle one.

"And I started first, and finished first," said the youngest.

The women began to argue. The old man sat and listened.

And the river rocked the boat and rocked the boat, then turned it around and carried it downstream.

The women kept arguing and saw nothing around them.

"I rowed first," cried the youngest. "And I won't be the last as well! Let the one who followed me take the oars."

"I was in the middle, and there I'll stay," cried the second one.

"Do you expect me to take two turns at a time?" cried the eldest.

In the meantime the boat floated and floated downstream, till their village came in sight. And then the women turned on the old man and shouted all together:

"Where were you? What were you doing all this time? Why are we back where we started?"

But the old man laughed.

"Each one of you finished her turn, so the river went to work for you. It didn't care whose turn it was. But you can't tell a river to carry a boat upstream. It took you wherever it was going. You'd better get ashore now before we pass our village."

And so they came home without fish.

The old man has long forgotten all about it. But the women still argue whose turn it was at the oars.

Three Knots

There was a man who had a marvelously lazy son. All day the son did nothing but sail up and down the river in a bucket. The boy's mother and father scolded and shouted and whipped him, but nothing helped. He would do nothing but sail up and down.

One day the mother said to the father:

"We must find a sailor to teach our son the sailing craft. Then he can go off on a ship and earn his bread. All our scolding and our whipping does him no good anyway."

They found a sailor who took the boy as an apprentice. The father bought them a ship and the two went off on a journey. When they came out into the open sea, the boy asked:

"What shall I do if a storm breaks? I don't know how to sail a ship."

The old seaman took a cord with three knots from his pocket and said to the young man:

"If you untie the first knot, a storm will rise and sweep the

sea upon the shore. If you untie the second knot, the waves will fall, the sea will be as quiet as a lake. If you untie the third knot, the wind will blow in any direction you may wish."

One day they sailed into a harbor where many other ships lay at anchor waiting for a wind to fill their sails. The young sailor went ashore to stretch his legs and met a prince. The prince looked very sad and kept sighing.

"What ails you?" asked the sailor.

"I am engaged to a beautiful princess," said the prince. "Tomorrow is our wedding day, and there is still no wind. If I do not return in time, my princess will be married to another."

The sailor told him not to grieve, he'd be with his betrothed in good time. They got into the waiting ship. The sailor untied the third knot. A fair wind rose, and they sped off. By evening the prince was with his princess. And when the sailor was about to leave, the prince gave him a letter to his father, the old king.

It just so happened that when the sailor arrived the old king was giving a great feast for all the knights and princes who had come to woo his daughter, one of the loveliest girls in the world. The guests ate, drank, and were merry, and no one went to bed till late at night. But when they wakened in the morning, they found the princess gone. She had been stolen by one of her suitors and carried off to a distant island. The other suitors mourned, the old king moaned and wept.

"Don't weep, king," said the sailor. "We shall find your daughter. Get into my ship and we'll set off in search of her."

He untied the third knot and the ship sailed off with the wind. And soon they reached the island where the princess had been taken. The sailor anchored his ship and untied the first knot. A frightful storm arose, the waves grew high as mountains, they swept upon the shore and threatened to flood the island. Everybody hurried to the ship, but the sailor would let no one get aboard until they brought the princess. Then he untied the second knot, the waves lay down like lambs, and the sea became smooth as a lake. The islanders were no longer afraid and went back to their homes, and the ship set out on the return journey. Again the sailor untied the third knot, and the ship flew home with the fair wind like a white-winged bird.

The king rejoiced to have his daughter back. He ordered the greatest feast his land had ever seen, and gave the princess to the sailor as his bride. And, because the king was old and tired, he gave him the kingdom as well.

The sailor, who was now king, ruled well and wisely, and found proper occupations for all the lazies of his land, for he had learned from his own experience that no man will be lazy if he finds the thing he truly likes to do.

And once every year, the king would take his queen and children and the magic cord, and board his ship, and visit his old parents and his brother-in-law, the prince. And do you think he did this only because he longed to see them all again? No, there was another reason as well. For though he was no longer lazy, he still liked sailing up and down and up and down the waters most of all.

As for the old sailor who had taught him his craft, he turned out to be a great magician whose home was in the sea. One day he came to the king and said:

"Good-by, my friend, my work is done."

And with those words he plunged into the waves, turned into sea foam, and was seen no more.

Two Frogs

A RUSSIAN TALE

Two frogs lived in the pond near a peasant's house. One day they poked their heads out of the water and saw a pot of cream standing near the porch. They hopped over and jumped in to see what kind of white water this was. But then they could not jump out, for the pot was deep and the cream was thicker than water. One of the frogs said to himself:

"Well, this is my last day. I'll drown, and nothing I can do will save me. There's no use trying."

And he sank down to the bottom and drowned.

But the other frog wasn't lazy, and he did not want to die. He said to himself:

"I may die in the end, but first I will do all I can to get out of this trouble."

26

And he swam, and he kicked, and he thrashed about till he had hardly any more strength to go on. And yet he did go on and on. Then suddenly, when he was almost losing hope, he felt something hard and slippery under his feet. He looked down—and there was a firm yellow ball in the pot: he had churned the cream so long that it had turned to butter. And the frog jumped out of the pot and quickly skipped back to his pond. But his friend who would not try lay dead in the pot until the peasant threw him out on the garbage heap.

The Clever Thief

A LATVIAN TALE

Once there lived a young man who was his parents' only son. They spoiled and petted him and never taught him any work. And the boy grew up lazy, without any skill or trade. One day the father said to his son:

"It's time for you to earn your own bread."

"You've fed me, Father, until now," said the son. "Feed me another year."

A year later the same thing happened. And two years later. The third year the father told his son again:

"It's time, my son, for you to earn your own bread."

But the son replied:

"How can I earn my bread, Father, if you've never taught me anything? I've grown up ignorant and lazy. What can I do if there is nothing I can do?"

His father finally went to the king to complain about his son. The king commanded the young man to be brought to the palace.

"Why don't you go to work?" asked the king.

"How can I work if my father has brought me up ignorant and lazy?"

"Well," said the king in anger. "If you can't earn a living for yourself and your old parents by honest labor, you'll have to become a thief."

And the king walked out and slammed the door.

This was the day for the king to take his monthly bath. He went to the bathhouse and left his boots outside. The lazy young man crept up and made off with the boots.

In the morning the king called the young man:

"Hey, you stole my boots!"

"Why not? Wasn't it you who told me to become a thief?"

The king burst out laughing and said:

"So you've really decided to live by stealing?"

"I have," said the young man.

Now I must test him, thought the king, and have some fun as well.

"All right," he said. "Let me see if you can steal my black horse tonight. If you do, I shall give you enough money to feed your parents for the rest of their lives."

The young man walked out, but, as he was leaving, he saw the king's old caftan in the hallway, and he carried it off. The king commanded his grooms not to sleep that night, for somebody was plotting to steal his black horse. The grooms promised to guard the horse well. When darkness

fell, the lazy son put on the king's caftan, came to the stable
door, and shouted:

"Where is my black horse? I must chase a thief!"

The grooms were too sleepy to realize this was a stranger's
voice. They saw the king's glittering caftan and brought the
horse from the stable.

In the morning the king asked his grooms:

"Where is my black horse? Was it stolen last night?"

But the grooms could only stand and gape. And the lazy
son rode proudly into the yard and cried:

"You see, I've earned my parents' bread."

The king paid him as handsomely as he had promised and said:

"Now let me see if you are clever enough to steal one of my cows. If you do, you'll be rewarded even better than before."

Next morning, the king commanded his best shepherd:

"Don't leave the meadow, and watch well. See that no thief steals any of my cows."

That evening, the lazy son had snared a pheasant and hid with it under a bush right near the pasture. The shepherd sat and watched his herd. Then he got tired of sitting, and took a walk through the herd to see that everything was well. When he came near the bush, the young man let the pheasant go. "Oh, what a splendid bird!" cried the shepherd and ran after it—for it would make a fine dish for the king.

Meantime, the young man tied the muzzle of the brindled

cow with his belt so that she would not low, and led her away.

The king kept his word and paid the young man well. Then he said:

"I see you are a clever young man. Will you stay in my palace and be the overseer of all my goods and men?"

But the young man was still a lazy fellow, and he answered:

"No, I will not, although I thank you for the honor. I have a fine black horse. I have a brindled cow. And I have money enough to feed my parents and myself, and even a wife if I should choose to take one. I do not have to work, I do not have to steal. I'll go back to my own house and live my own life."

He bowed to the king and left the palace well rewarded. And the king was also pleased, for he had had his money's worth of fun.

The Ox and the Ass

AN UYGUR TALE

A man who understood animal language owned two oxen and an ass. One day he heard the ass mocking the oxen.

"You stupid beasts! Why do you toil all day long in the fields for a bundle of hay? You'll work so hard you will become all skin and bones, or even die of exhaustion. Now look at me—I do the easy work around the house and live like a lord."

"What can we do about it?" asked the oxen.

"It's easy," said the ass. "Work a day or two, and then let one of you pretend that he is sick. If they bring you hay, don't eat it. If they give you water, don't drink it. And if the master takes you out to harness you, limp as you walk. Then he will leave you home, and you can lead an easy life like me."

Two days later one of the oxen began to limp. He would not eat, he would not drink, he only bellowed piteously.

"How lucky that I have an ass," said the master, watching the ox with sympathy. "I'll harness him in place of the sick ox."

And all that day the ass pulled at the plow with the other ox. By evening he was so exhausted that his ears hung down and his legs were trembling so that he could barely walk. He limped to the stall, and did not even touch the hay his master had prepared for him.

The master in the meantime stood outside the stall to see what would happen.

"What is the trouble, ass?" the sick ox asked. "You look so downcast, and your legs tremble, and your ears no longer stand up. And you won't even take a bite of food."

"Oh, my good friend," replied the ass. "I heard a terrible thing today. I meant to do you a good turn, but I'm afraid I may unwittingly become the cause of your death. Our master told the butcher today, 'My ox is very sick. If he does not recover by tomorrow, I'll have to slaughter him for meat.' That's why I look so sad, and why my ears hang down and my legs tremble."

"What shall I do now?" cried the frightened ox.

"Don't worry," the ass replied. "I got you into this, and I will save you. Just get well. Eat your hay and drink your water. Stop limping. And when our master sees you working in the field, he will not think of slaughtering you any more."

The master heard them and began to laugh. "Who said an ass is stupid?"

The Princess Who Learned to Work

AN ARMENIAN TALE

A poor young peasant lived in a small village with his mother. All they owned was their hut, a strip of land, and two oxen. In the spring they harnessed the oxen and plowed their field. In the fall they took their crops to market. And so they always had enough to eat. But one day misfortune struck: one of their oxen died.

Spring came, time to plow the land, but how could they plow with a single ox? And they had no money to buy a second one. Then the mother said:

"I'll get into the yoke with the ox, and you will push the plow."

Just at that time the czar was riding in the nearby wood. He came into the field with his attendant and stopped in wonder at the strange sight.

"Call the young man, I want to talk to him," he said to the attendant.

And when the peasant approached, the czar began to scold him:

"Aren't you ashamed, driving an old woman up and down the field as if she were a beast?"

"Do not be angry, Your Majesty. We are poor people. We lost our second ox last winter, and if we do not plow the field we shall die of hunger."

"Unharness her at once!" cried the czar. "I'll send you a small bullock from my herds. If you can put him to the yoke, you may keep him as a present from me. And good luck to you."

The next day the bullock was brought to the peasant. But it was not a bullock at all—it was a huge, raging bull that needed five strong men to keep him in check.

"No matter," said the young man. "I'll handle him somehow."

He tied him up in the stall and kept him for three days without food. The bull snorted and bellowed day and night, but by the fourth day he began to quiet down a little, and the peasant brought him a pail of water and an armful of hay.

By the sixth day the bull was tame enough to be harnessed to the yoke and taken into the field to plow. And after he had done a good day's work, he was given a nice big meal.

The czar came over to see what happened and was amazed to see his savage bull pulling the plow.

"How did you tame that bull?" he asked.

"Well, as you see, I managed," the peasant answered with a grin.

"In that case," said the czar, "hear what I have to say. I have a lovely daughter, but she gives me no end of trouble. She is so lazy that nobody can make her lift a finger. She sits by the window all day and will not move from the spot. If you could teach that bull to work, you surely will be able to teach my daughter to be a good wife. Why don't you marry her?"

"Why not?" said the young peasant.

Before long they celebrated the wedding, and the lazy princess went to live in the peasant's hut. In the morning she got up, sat down by the window, folded her arms, and stayed there looking out all day.

The mother chided her son:

"Whom did you bring into our home, my son? We don't need such a lazybones."

"Don't worry," said the young man. "She will learn."

That evening he gave his wife no food or drink, not even bread or water.

"My mother and I work hard from dawn to dusk," he said to her. "We earn our bread, and you just sit there with folded arms. Why should we feed you?"

The next day the czar's daughter got up from the bench, swept the floor under her feet, and sat down again.

In the evening the son said to the mother:

"Give her some water and a little piece of bread."

On the third day the girl swept half the floor, and sat down again. In the evening her husband gave her two pieces of bread.

"What a terrible house," the girl thought. "At home I got the finest food without doing anything, and here they make me work."

But there was nothing to be done about it. After all, she did not want to starve to death! And little by little she learned to clean the house and sweep the yard and sew and cook. And she sat at the table with her husband and his mother and ate everything they did.

One day the czar decided to visit his daughter. "I'll go and see how my lazybones is doing."

He took some presents with him and rode to the village.

Imagine his amazement when his daughter ran out to meet him, helped him down, tied up his horse, and gave it hay and water. Then she led her father into the house.

"Sit down," she said, "and help me. I am preparing supper, and you can peel and chop some garlic for me."

The czar grinned to himself, but he said nothing and went to work.

When the old woman came home she found them busy at their tasks.

"What is this, daughter?" she cried. "Making the czar himself peel garlic?"

"Naturally," said the girl. "Otherwise you will not give him anything to eat!"

Toast and Honey

A MOLDAVIAN TALE

In a certain village there lived a man who was so lazy that he would not even chew his food, but swallowed it in lumps. And since he did no work, his family and neighbors had to feed and clothe him. They argued with him, and they shamed him, and they scolded him, but nothing helped. At last they wearied of the idler and decided to play a trick on him and teach him a lesson.

Two villagers came to his home, lifted him from the bench on which he lay all day and night, and threw him into a cart.

"We are going to drown you," they said, and drove off to the river.

He yawned, and did not even move to make himself more comfortable in the cart.

On the way they met a lady in a fine carriage.

"Good people," she asked, "is the poor fellow sick?"

"He isn't sick," one of the peasants answered. "But he's the laziest man the world has ever known. He will not sow,

he will not reap, he will not do a thing. So we've decided to drown him in the river and rid the village of such a good-for-nothing."

"Oh, no," the kindly lady cried. "How can you drown a living man? You'd better bring him over to my estate. It's just beyond that hill. I have a barn full of toasted bread, stocked for a rainy day. Let him eat the toast and live in peace. No one will be the poorer for it. We must help each other."

"Did you hear that?" the peasants asked the idler. "You're in luck, the lady wants to save your worthless life. Get out and thank her, and be off with you. And make it quick, we've no more time to waste on you!"

But the idler did not even turn his head. He squinted over at the lady and asked:

"And what about the honey?"

"What did he say?" the lady asked.

"He wants to know about the honey."

"What honey?"

"Toast is too hard to chew," the idler said. "Will it be dipped in honey?"

"I've never heard of such a thing!" the lady said, marveling. "Can't he eat toast without honey?"

"Well, if she won't send somebody to dip the toast in

honey, I can't be bothered," the idler mumbled and yawned again. "Just drive on."

And so the peasants went on to the river. They lifted the idler from the cart, threw him into the water, and drove away. But he was so lazy that he would not even move a limb to swim or climb out onto the bank. Down and down he went, like a stone, and lay there on the bottom until the breath went out of him.

The Bird, the Mouse, and the Sausage

A LATVIAN TALE

A bird, a mouse, and a sausage lived together in a tiny hut. They lived in peace and harmony, and each had his own work to do. The bird gathered firewood, the mouse carried water from the well, and the sausage did the cooking. Every day before dinnertime the bird would fly into the woods and bring twigs for the fire; the mouse would bring water; and the sausage would jump into the pot of soup, dip itself in it

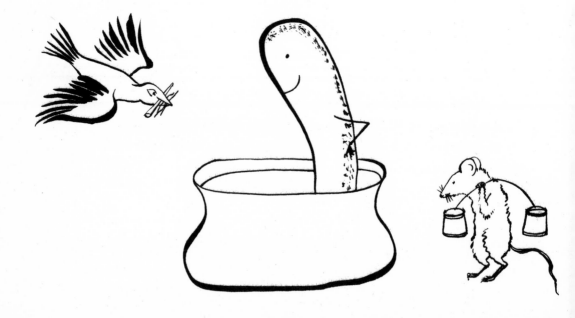

three times, and jump out. And so the sausage remained whole, and the friends had a delicious soup for their dinner.

They lived together for a long time, until one day the bird refused to fly into the wood for twigs.

"Why must I do all the hard work," he said, "while you lead easy lives?"

"And the mouse said: "Why must I always carry heavy pails of water while you lead easy lives?"

And the sausage said: "Why must I always jump into hot soup while you lead easy lives?"

They started quarreling, and none of them would do any more work.

A day passed, and another, and a third, and they got hungrier and hungrier. Then they decided to take turns at each task, so none would feel that he was working harder than the others.

The sausage rolled to the woods for twigs. Before it got there, a dog caught it and snapped it up. The bird went to the well for water. When he was pulling up the pail, he slipped, fell into the well, and drowned. And the mouse stayed home to cook the soup. When the pot began to boil, she jumped in, as the sausage always did. She gave one squeak, and that was the end of the mouse.

The soup boiled away, the little hut burned down, and I, who saw it all, came here to tell the tale, if you will listen.

The Lazy Daughter

A KARELIAN TALE

In a faraway land there lived an old man and an old woman. They had only one daughter. The girl was as lovely as the sun, but so lazy that she would not do a single thing. The old man died. And the poor old mother had to go begging to feed herself and her daughter. One day the mother came home with a bag of crusts, but the daughter had spent all day lying on the stove and had not even brought some water from the well to soak the crusts. This time the mother lost all patience. She scolded the daughter and shouted at her so loudly that she could be heard even in the woods.

Just then the king's son was hunting in the woods. He heard the noise and came to see what it was all about. He found the girl lying on the stove, and the old woman screaming.

"What's all this shouting about?" he asked.

"How can I help but shout?" cried the old woman. "This girl of mine works so hard she will age before her time. I

49

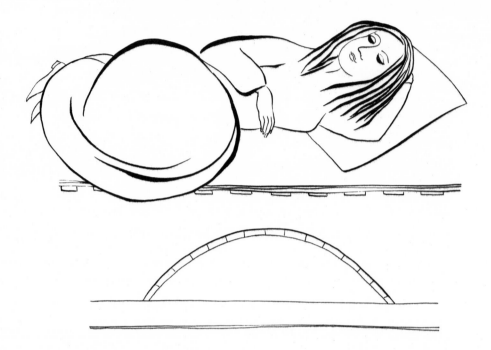

bring a bag of flax from the village, and she spins it all in a single day."

A few days later the old woman was scolding her daughter again for her laziness when the king's son was passing by, and he came into the house.

"What's all this shouting about now?"

"How can I help but shout?" cried the old woman. "This girl of mine works so hard she will age before her time. I bring a bag of flax from the village, and she spins it all in a single day. And then she works all night and weaves it into the finest cloth by morning, without a wink of sleep."

A few days later the old woman was scolding her daughter again when the king's son passed by, and came into the house.

"What's all the shouting about this time?"

"How can I help but shout?" cried the old woman. "This girl of mine works so hard she will age before her time. I bring a bag of flax from the village, and she spins it all in a single day. And then she works all night and weaves it into the finest cloth by morning, without a wink of sleep. And on the next day she cuts and sews the cloth into a splendid shirt, and embroiders it so beautifully it is fit for a king's son. I have no strength to run around supplying everything she needs for all that work."

Well, thought the king's son. The girl is beautiful and hard-working. Where can I find a better bride? I'll marry her and take her home to my father's palace.

He bought his future bride the finest silk and velvet clothes and shining jewels, and took her home with him. And the old mother went into a dance because she had lied so cleverly and got the lazy daughter off her hands.

It was the holiday season, and the king's son had many feasts to attend and many cousins to visit before his wedding could be celebrated. Since it was not proper to take his betrothed with him before they were married, he went off to the feasts without her. And each time he would leave the girl some task to keep her from getting bored and lonely.

The first time he brought her a bag of flax to spin into fine thread. After he left, the poor girl wept with fright. She did not know how to spin. Suddenly a horrible old crone appeared before her:

"If you'll invite me to your wedding, I will spin the flax for you."

The girl promised, and before she knew it, the woman had spun the flax into the strongest, silkiest thread. When the king's son and the courtiers returned from the feast, they could not stop praising the young woman's skill.

On the second day, the king's son and his retinue went to another feast, and he told the girl to weave the thread into fine cloth to keep from getting bored and lonely. After they left, another crone appeared, even more frightening than the first:

"If you'll invite me to your wedding, I will weave the thread for you."

On the third day, the king's son told the girl to make him a shirt. After he left, a third crone, the most terrifying of them all, appeared and offered to sew and embroider the shirt, if she too were invited to the wedding.

The girl promised and asked:

"Where will I find you and your sisters?"

"At the end of the field there is a mountain. Knock on the stone at its foot, and we shall come out from under it."

The shirt was beautiful enough to get married in. And after everyone admired it, the king's son decided it was time for the wedding.

Everybody got busy preparing a great feast, and the king and queen said to the girl:

"If you have relatives, invite them to the wedding."

"I have three aunts," said the girl. "I should invite them, but they are horrible to look at."

Still, if they had to be invited, they had to be invited. The girl went to the foot of the mountain and knocked on the stone. The three old crones came out from under it and went to the palace with the girl.

When the first old crone came in, the people stared at her and asked:

"What is the matter with her?"

And the crone said:

"I can neither sit nor stand, my leg won't listen to me." And her leg kept kicking out and kicking out by itself.

"How did it happen?" asked the people.

"I have been spinning all my life, pushing the wheel with my foot, and now I can't stop it from kicking."

The king's son looked at the old woman and thought: "If that's what spinning does to you, I'll never let my wife spin any more."

The next old woman was still more frightful. Her head kept turning from side to side, and her hands kept jerking and jerking.

"What is the matter with her?" asked the guests.

"I'm sorry, my good people," said the crone. "I've been weaving all my life, and now I cannot stop my head and hands from jerking all the time."

The king's son looked at the old woman and thought: "Oh, no, I'll never let my lovely wife weave any more."

And then the third crone came, and she was still more frightful than the first two. Her back was bent, her tongue lolled out of her mouth, and her eyes were red and bulging.

"What is the matter with her?" asked the people.

"Forgive me, good people," said the old crone. "I know I am not pleasant to look at. But I have been sewing and embroidering all my life, and so my back got bent, my tongue lolled out from licking the thread to get it into the needle's eye, and my eyes are bulging with the strain."

The king's son looked at the third woman and thought to himself: "Oh, no, I'll never let my lovely wife embroider or sew any more."

And then he married the lovely young girl and she lived like a queen and never had to work, and nobody, not even her husband, ever suspected that she was the laziest girl in the world.

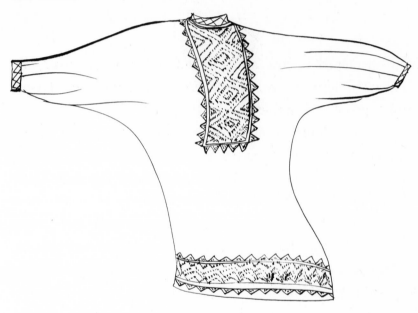

Ea and Eo

A CENTRAL ASIAN TALE

Ahmed owned a store and two donkeys, one gray and one black. The gray always brayed E-e-ea, and the black E-e-eo, and so people called them Ea and Eo.

One day Ahmed went with his donkeys to market to buy salt for his store. He loaded Ea and Eo with bags of salt and turned homeward. The salt was heavy, the day hot. Little black Eo walked as fast as he could, thinking:

"The quicker we go, the sooner we'll get home."

But little gray Ea stopped and dawdled on the way. He did not feel like carrying the load at all and he kept wondering how to get rid of it.

Soon they came to a bridge over a stream. Eo trotted across and stopped to wait for Ea and their master. But Ea took a sudden leap and landed right in the middle of the stream. The water was up to his neck, it was cool and pleasant, and he refused to budge. Ahmed called and shouted. Eo brayed: "E-e-eo, e-e-eo! Come on!" But Ea would not move. He stood there, and his load was getting lighter and lighter as the water washed away the salt. When all the salt was

gone, Ea jumped out of the water, the empty sacks dangling at his side, and merrily ran home, while Eo trudged behind with his load.

A few days later Ahmed went to market with his donkeys to buy blankets for his store. He bought many blankets— blue, and green, and red, and yellow—and loaded them on Ea and Eo. And the little caravan turned homeward. As always, Eo walked steadily, but Ea shook himself, kicked, stopped to nibble grass, and kept wondering how to get rid of his pack.

And when they came to the stream, he remembered the salt and said to himself: "E-e-ea! I know what I'll do!" And he leaped right into the water again. Again no threats or pleas or shouts could make him budge.

The stream was cool and pleasant. But this time the load refused to disappear. The blankets soaked up water, they got heavier and heavier, and poor Ea began to sag under their weight. Another moment and he would go under.

"E-e-ea!" he cried and tried to scramble out, but his feet sank deeper in the mud and he could not move.

Then Ahmed jumped into the stream and pushed and pulled until he managed to get Ea out of the water. Now little black Eo ran merrily ahead with the light, fluffy blankets —blue, and green, and red, and yellow. And Ea trudged behind him, panting under his heavy, dripping load that was no longer blue and green and red and yellow, but as gray and muddy as the lazy Ea himself.

Ayoga

A NANAY TALE

In a small village there was a girl called Ayoga. She was very pretty, and everybody liked her. But one day a neighbor said that Ayoga was the most beautiful girl for miles around. And Ayoga became very proud of herself. This was a long, long time ago, and nobody had mirrors in that little village in the northern woods. And so Ayoga would spend the whole day admiring her reflection in a shiny copper tray, or in the water of the lake. She stopped helping her mother. She wouldn't pick berries, she wouldn't bring firewood, she wouldn't sweep the floor. And soon the neighbors began to say that Ayoga was the laziest girl for miles around.

One day her mother said:

"Bring me some water, Ayoga."

But Ayoga answered:

"I'll fall into the lake."

"Hold on to a bush."

"The bush will break."

"Pick a strong one."

"I'll scratch my hands."

"Put on mittens."

"They'll tear," said Ayoga. And all the time she kept look-ing at herself in the copper tray, thinking, How beautiful I am!

"If the mittens tear," said her mother, "you can mend them."

"The needle will break."

"Find a thick one."

"I'll prick my finger."

"Use a thimble."

"The thimble will crack," answered Ayoga, and would not stir.

Then the girl who lived next door said:

"I will bring you water."

The girl went down to the lake and brought the water.

Ayoga's mother mixed the water with flour, shaped the dough into pancakes, and baked them in the hot stove. When Ayoga saw the steaming pancakes, she cried:

"Give me a pancake, Mother!"

"It's hot, you'll burn your hands."

"I'll put on mittens."

"The mittens are wet."

"I'll dry them in the sun!"

"They'll shrink and stiffen."

"I'll stretch them! I'll pound them till they are soft again!"

"Your hands will get tired," said her mother. "Why should you work and spoil your beauty? I'll give the pancake to the girl who doesn't think so much about her hands."

And the mother gave the pancake to the girl who brought the water.

Ayoga was very angry and ran away to the lake. She looked down at her reflection in the water and admired herself. And the other girl sat down nearby, munching her pancake. Ayoga kept turning her head to look at the girl, and her neck stretched out and grew longer and longer. Then the girl said to Ayoga:

"Here, Ayoga! Take a piece of pancake, I don't mind."

But this made Ayoga still angrier. She was white with rage. Why should she, the most beautiful girl for miles around, eat somebody else's leavings? She spread her fingers and waved away the girl and her pancake. She waved and waved until her arms turned into wings.

"S-s-s-s!" she hissed. "I don't need your nasty pancake! Go away, go away, go-go-go!"

She waved and waved until she lost her balance and went plop! into the water. She hissed and flapped her wings and swam about, and turned into a big, white goose. And still she cried:

"Oh, how beautiful I am! Go-go-go! How beautiful! Ga-ga-ga!"

Nobody expected her to work now. All she did was swim about in the lake, crying "Go-go-go!" and "Ga-ga-ga!" till she forgot all human words. The only word she remembered was her own name—"Ayoga."

And to this day, to make sure that no one will confuse the beautiful Ayoga with anybody else, she still cries to every man or beast that passes by:

"Ay-o-ga-ga-ga! Ay-o-ga-ga-ga!"

The Miller's Sons

AN AVAR TALE

Once upon a time there lived a miller. His mill stood over a rapid stream, and the miller knew his work well. He worked hard and never complained of his lot. And because he was a miller, his beard was always white with flour.

But one day the miller died. And his three sons began to argue about their inheritance.

The two elder brothers wanted to divide it. The youngest tried to convince them to work together. But they were too stubborn to be convinced and too lazy to work.

"I do not want to work at the mill like our father and walk about with flour in my beard," said the elder. And so he rejected the mill and chose the pond for himself.

"I will not go about with a dusty beard either," said the middle brother, and chose the roof of the mill.

And so the mill and all the work were left to the younger brother.

The elder brother cleared the pond, the middle brother fixed the roof, and that was all the work they did. But the youngest toiled at the mill from dawn to dusk, grinding grain into flour for the people.

After a while the elder brother got tired of bothering with the pond. He threw away his spade and left.

He walked a long time. He passed one mountain, then another, until he came to the gorge where the dragon Ashdaga lived.

"Good morning, Ashdaga," he said, bowing and trembling with fear.

"Huh, what a polite guest I have!" grumbled Ashdaga and asked: "Do you know a story or a song to entertain me with?"

"No," said the elder brother, "I don't know any."

"You don't? Then I will eat you," said the dragon, and he gulped him down.

Some time later, when the mill roof needed more repairs, the middle brother also went away. He, too, came to the dragon and ended up in its belly.

But the youngest was a good and loyal brother. He could not stay home and grind flour when his two brothers had disappeared. He stopped the mill, opened the dam of the pond, and went out to look for them. He walked and walked until he came to the gorge where Ashdaga lived. He saw the dragon's round belly and realized at once what had happened to his brothers.

"Greetings to you, Ashdaga!" he cried. "Greetings as wide and as deep as your canyon."

"Huh, what a civil guest I have," mumbled Ashdaga. "But tell me, do you know any tales or songs to entertain me with?"

"I certainly do! I know songs, I know stories, and I know a thing or two besides. If you wish, I will sing. If you wish, I will tell you a story. And if there is anything else you wish, I'll do that too."

"Start with a story," commanded Ashdaga.

"Very well! But till I finish my story, Ashdaga, you must say neither 'yes' nor 'no.' If you say a single word, I'll rip open your belly. Agreed?"

"Agreed," said Ashdaga, and the miller began:

"I had fifty horses. During the summer, when I took them out to graze, it became very hot, and all the water everywhere dried up. The little foals were very thirsty, so I drove them to the river. But the river was covered with a thick coat of ice, and the foals could not drink. Then I took my ax from my belt and chopped a hole in the ice. 'Poor river,' I thought. 'It must feel cold. I'll have to warm it up.' I went to the woods, gathered some firewood, and made a fire. But

a great misfortune happened: the river caught fire, and then the rocks along the bank. I wanted to chop more holes in the ice and get some water to put out the fire, but I had lost my ax. When I found it, I saw that the iron was burned to a crisp, and only the wooden handle remained."

Ashdaga wanted to say, "No, iron doesn't burn," but he remembered the agreement and kept silent.

"My horses ran away," went on the miller, "so I went back to the woods to build myself a cart. With the ax handle, I chopped down some trees and built the cart. Then I got hungry and shot two deer with the ax handle. I ate the meat and hung the skins on branches to dry out.

"A while later I went to see how they were drying and found two bees fighting under the tree. Each shouted that it gathered more honey than the other.

" 'Don't fight,' I said to them. 'It's easy to decide who is right without quarreling. Fly out now and bring me honey, and I will tell you who collected more.'

"The bees went out for honey, hurrying to see who would bring more. In a few days both deerskins were full.

" 'You see,' I said to them. 'Each of you collected as much honey as the other, and so there was no need for you to fight.'

"Since my horses were gone, I harnessed the two bees to

my cart, piled the deerskins filled with honey into it, and climbed in myself.

"The bees pulled the cart strongly and smoothly, and I didn't have to lash them. But suddenly one of them stumbled. I swung my whip, but it got tangled in a cloud and I was thrown up high into the sky. I caught at the edge of the cloud with one hand and hung there for a long time, until I saw a haystack on the ground and jumped right into it. . . ."

"No!" cried Ashdaga, unable to keep quiet any longer. "It's all a pack of lies! Such things don't happen."

"Put out your belly, dragon!" shouted the miller, and with a single blow of his dagger he ripped Ashdaga's belly open.

And that very second his older brothers jumped out, pale and thin, but very happy.

They danced to celebrate their liberation, and then all three returned to the mill and went to work in peace and harmony, never refusing any task and never worrying again because their beards were white with flour.